Eleanor Roosevelt
and the Scary Basement

written by Peter Merchant
illustrated by Anna DiVito

Ready-to-Read • Aladdin
New York London Toronto Sydney

To Dick Banker —P. M.
For Alicia and Saskia —A. D.

ALADDIN PAPERBACKS
An imprint of Simon & Schuster Children's Publishing Division
1230 Avenue of the Americas, New York, NY 10020

Designed by Lisa Vega
The text of this book was set in Century Oldstyle BT.
Manufactured in the United States of America
First Aladdin Paperbacks edition November 2006
2 4 6 8 10 9 7 5 3 1
Library of Congress Cataloging-in-Publication Data
Merchant, Peter.
Eleanor Roosevelt and the scary basement / by Peter Merchant ; illustrated by Anna DiVito.
p. cm. — (Ready-to-read. Level 2) (Childhood of famous Americans)
ISBN-13: 978-0-689-87205-1 ISBN-10: 0-689-87205-4 (pbk.)
ISBN-13: 978-0-689-87206-8 ISBN-10: 0-689-87206-2 (library ed.)
1. Roosevelt, Eleanor, 1884-1962—Childhood and youth—Juvenile literature. 2. Presidents' spouses—United States—Biography—Juvenile literature. 3. Fear of the dark—United States—Juvenile literature. I. DiVito, Anna, ill. II. Title. III. Series. IV. Series: Childhood of famous Americans series.
E807.1.R48M47 2006 973.917092—dc22 2005034201

When she was a little girl,
Eleanor Roosevelt was scared
of everything.

She never felt pretty.

Eleanor was scared of being seen

at all, by anyone.

Eleanor was scared of boats.

She was afraid of falling into the water.

She was scared of mice.

She was scared of horses.

She was scared of robbers.

But most of all,
Eleanor was scared of the dark.
This was a problem,
since she lived in a
very dark house.

Still, Eleanor liked her home.

Her aunt Edith

lived there too.

Eleanor loved Aunt Edith,

and loved to please her.

One night,

after everyone had gone to sleep,

Eleanor's aunt called out for her.

"Eleanor!" she cried out in the dark.

"Oh, Eleanor!"

Eleanor opened her eyes.

She did not want to get out of bed,

but she could not ignore her aunt.

She knew what she must do.

Eleanor crept through the dark
very slowly,
shaking all the way
to Aunt Edith's room.

There in the dark room
lay her dear aunt.
She looked very sick.
"Eleanor," she said in a scratchy voice,
"could you fetch me some ice, dear?
My throat is so very sore.
A little ice water would soothe my pain."
Eleanor froze.
How could she get ice for her aunt?
That would mean going downstairs,
into the darkest room in the house:
the basement!

But Eleanor loved her aunt.
She knew what she must do.
Taking a deep breath,
she lit a candle,
picked up the ice bucket,
and crept down the hall.

When she got to the basement door,
Eleanor stopped.
She thought she heard a noise–
and it was coming from the basement!
Maybe she should turn around.
But then . . . what would her aunt say?

Slowly, Eleanor opened the door
to the basement.
It was so dark, so quiet.
She wanted to turn back.
But, with her heart beating fast,
she tiptoed down the stairs.

At the bottom step
Eleanor heard another noise,
like scratching.
This time, she knew it was real.
Moving her candle toward the noise,
she saw something:

A rat!

It dropped to the floor with a *thud*,

then rushed off into a corner,

out of sight.

Eleanor took a deep breath.

She had made it this far.

She had to bring back some ice.

But she had a new problem:

She did not know

where the icebox was.

Not exactly.

And it was very, very dark . . .

Slowly, Eleanor moved
to the back of the basement.
She found a small door
opened just a crack.
Standing in front of the door,
she felt a sudden chill.
Was someone there?

Eleanor wanted to leave,
but she couldn't go
without the ice.
Taking another breath,
she opened the small door
to a smaller room.

The icebox!

As she opened the icebox,
Eleanor felt something sticky
all over her face.
"Spiders!" yelled Eleanor.

As she clawed at the spiderweb,
she dropped her bucket
and her candle.
The flame went out.

Now, it was darker than ever,

but Eleanor did not run.

She had made it so far,

and her aunt needed her.

There was only one thing

for her to do.

She picked up the bucket

and filled it up with ice.

On her way back to the basement door,
Eleanor bumped into some things.
They made her heart jump.
But she made it out
with a full bucket of ice!

Grinning,
Eleanor skipped up the stairs
to her aunt's room.

“Eleanor!” said her aunt.

“I was starting to worry about you.

The dark can be very scary.”

“Oh,” said Eleanor, “do not worry about me.

I am fine!”

Eleanor proudly handed over the ice.

From that night on,
Eleanor was less afraid.
For the rest of her life,
she would always face her fears head-on.

Eleanor Roosevelt grew up

to be a hero.

She overcame her fear of people

to become a famous public speaker

and a bold first lady.

Eleanor never let her fears get in the way

of helping other people.

Here is a time line of Eleanor Roosevelt's life:

1884 Eleanor Roosevelt is born in New York City

1892 Eleanor's mother dies; Eleanor moves in with her grandmother

1894 Eleanor's father dies

1899 Eleanor is sent to boarding school in England

1905 Eleanor marries future president Franklin Roosevelt in New York City

1920 Eleanor joins the League of Women Voters, an organization devoted to women's right to vote

1924 Eleanor delivers the keynote speech at the Democratic National Convention

1932 Eleanor becomes first lady of the United States as her husband is elected president

1933 Eleanor initiates White House press conferences for women reporters; Eleanor becomes a champion of the poor, women, and African Americans

1939 Eleanor resigns from the Daughters of the American Revolution in protest against their racism

1945 Franklin Roosevelt dies; World War II ends

1946 Eleanor is asked to be among the first American delegates to the United Nations

1948 Eleanor helps pass the U.N. Universal Declaration of Human Rights

1962 Eleanor Roosevelt dies of a stroke